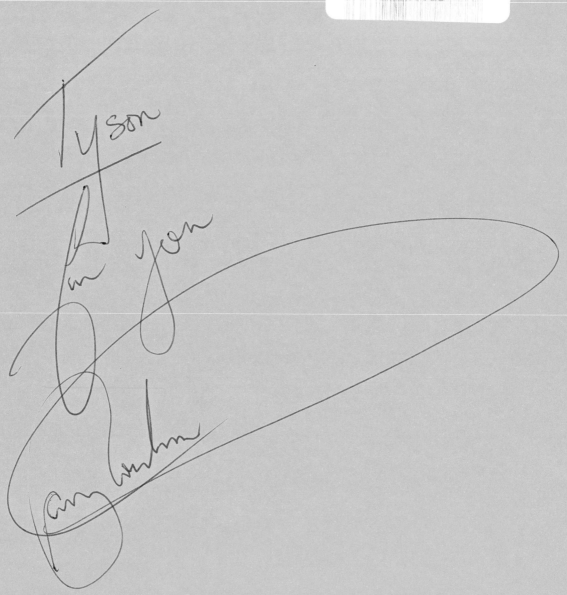

VOICES
FROM THE
WILD

AN ANIMAL
SENSAGORIA

SIGHT
SMELL
TOUCH
HEARING
TASTE

VOICES
FROM THE
WILD

AN ANIMAL
SENSAGORIA

David Bouchard
paintings by **Ron Parker**

Fitzhenry & Whiteside

Published in Canada by Fitzhenry & Whiteside,
195 Allstate Parkway, Markham, ON L3R 4T8

Published in the United States by Fitzhenry & Whiteside,
311 Washington Street, Brighton, Massachusetts 02135

Fitzhenry & Whiteside acknowledges with thanks the Canada Council for the Arts,
and the Ontario Arts Council for their support of our publishing program.
We acknowledge the financial support of the Government of Canada through
the Canada Book Fund (CBF) for our publishing activities.

ONTARIO ARTS COUNCIL
CONSEIL DES ARTS DE L'ONTARIO
an Ontario government agency
un organisme du gouvernement de l'Ontario

Canada Council   Conseil des arts
for the Arts   du Canada

Library and Archives Canada Cataloguing in Publication
Bouchard, David, 1952-, author
Voices from the wild : an animal sensagoria / David
Bouchard ; paintings by Ron Parker.
Originally published: Vancouver : Raincoast Books, 1996.
ISBN 978-1-55455-295-5 (bound)
1. Animals--Juvenile poetry. 2. Senses and sensation--
Juvenile poetry. 3. Children's poetry, Canadian (English).
I. Parker, Ron, illustrator II. Title.
PS8553.O759V6 2013   jC811'.54   C2013-903754-3

Publisher Cataloging-in-Publication Data (U.S.)
Bouchard, David.
Voices from the wild : an animal sensagoria / David Bouchard ; paintings by Ron Parker.
[72] p. : col. ill. ; cm.
Summary: A collection of poems classified into five sections:
sight, smell, touch, hearing, and taste, in which animals relate how they survive in the wild.
ISBN: 978-1-55455-295-5
1. Animals – Juvenile poetry. 2. Senses and sensation –Juvenile poetry. 3. Children's poetry, Canadian (English). I. Parker, Ron. II. Title.
811.6 dc23   PR9199.4.O759V643 2013

Printed and bound in China by Sheck Wah Tong Printing Press Ltd.

Although I wrote this book with young people in mind,
I would like to dedicate it to the memory of my uncle Adrien
whose No Hunting signs are still seen
on his fence 35 years after his death.

— D.B.

To my mother, Jessie Parker,
for her unending support and encouragement.

— R.P.

Grateful acknowledgement is made for permission to reproduce the following paintings:

Mill Pond Press, Inc., and Ron Parker for
Inside Passage (Orca)
Autumn Leaves (Red Fox)
Snow Palace (Mule Deer)
Resting Spot (Lynx)
Winter's Fury (Mountain Goat)
Low Water (Raccoon)
Autumn Foraging (Moose)
Just Resting (Sea Otter)
Icy Creek (Mink)
Rimrock (Cougar)

Wolf Creek Editions, and Ron Parker for
Crossing the Ridge (Wolf)

Greenwich Workshop, and Ron Parker for
Morning Flight (Bald Eagle)

Ron Parker, for all other paintings.

For information on Ron Parker's limited-edition fine art prints, please call 1-800-263-4001.
In the U.S., 1-800-243-4246. In the U.K., 1-684-311113.

Have you ever stopped to think
About each of nature's children?
Have you ever stopped to wonder
Who got what, and how and why?
Who was given the best of each sense?

Is the vision of the eagle
Any better than the cougar's?
Can the owl hear that much more
Than its prey, the nervous hare?
If all other things were equal,
Who could smell from greatest distance?
And if one would like to know,
Who to ask to find the answer?
What to ask and who would answer?

I know one who can be trusted.
I know one who's lived among them.
I know one who's spent his life
Near them watching, learning from them.

He can show us what he's learned.
He can paint for all a judgment.
Who sees farthest, who smells keenest,
Which from all those in his world
Has the sharpest sense of taste.
He can help us see and feel
Which has the softest touch of all.

He's the one that we can ask.
Go to him and have him choose.

SIGHT

BALD EAGLE

Look up here, northern painter.
I'm the one who soars above you,
I'm the ruler of the sky,
Royal hunter; proudly watching.

Are there others that you know of
Who from over two miles high
See the salmon in the river
As it glistens in the sun?

Can you speak of any other
Who can dive at breakneck speed
Always focused on his victim?

I can see you there below me.
I can see you crystal clear;
See the speck upon your cheek.

I have watched you down there painting
In the cold till night was on you.
I have often looked and wondered
If your motives were to harm us.
But with my keen eye I've seen
That you mean no harm against us.

Look up here, gentle painter!
I'm the one who soars above you.
Look way up and don't be frightened.
I'm the ruler of the sky,
Royal hunter, proudly watching.

He is one so easily noticed.
He is one who looks the part.
Yes , he soars in royal fashion,
Always wary; always ready.
While I sit here hunched and watching
Like the reaper stalking death.

Yet I too have strong, sharp vision,
Though few know that this is so.
Most think that I only *smell* death.
Here's a chance to tell my story.
Have Them know if not respect me,
Have Them come to see my purpose,
Have Them learn my sight's the best.

You could tell Them it's not often
That my victim's in the open.
You can show Them how I'm different,
How I perch and search for small things,
Almost always search for small things.

You can show Them through your painting,
How I live on sight *and* wit.

If They could, I'm sure They'd notice —
As can I, from far-off places —
Notice dozens of small black flies
Moving quickly behind bushes.
What could lie behind those branches?
So I move down from my lookout,
Down to see what could be hidden.
What could draw so many flies?

Most think that I only *smell* death
Here's a chance to tell my story.
Have Them know if not respect me,
Have Them come to see my purpose,
Have Them learn my sight's the best.

WHO is there who dares forget me?
WHO is there WHO dares not know me?
Know how dangerous is the old owl.
Know my vision in the dark.

WHO out there on land or water
Thinks they see the way I can?

Sit beside me for a moment
In this oak tree any night.
Choose a night in total blackness,
Any night — just sit and watch.

Can you see beside that rosebush,
Over down beyond the dark path?
Can you see it moving quickly,
That small mouse, it's there to feed me?
Can you see it? Try your hardest.
No, you can't. Of course you can't.

Could the eagle or the vulture?
No they couldn't, none else can.

Watch and listen while you paint me
As I hunt in blackest night.
Watch and listen, and then judge me
As the one whose eyes are keenest,
As the one who sees the best.

GREAT HORNED OWL

ADÉLIE PENGUIN

Please come closer, join the party.
Aren't you cold? You must be frozen.
Though you're not in your tuxedo,
You're quite welcome here with us.

You have some so far to meet us!
And you noted as you watched us
How we make our living fishing
In these freezing southern waters.

You've observed that we are flightless,
That we waddle and we huddle.
But have you noticed that we're gifted
When we dive and when we swim?

What you can't know just by looking
Is what makes our sight unique:
How we see beneath the ocean,
See through dark, concealing waters —
See what's lurking all around us
And in more than black and white.

We see hues of blues and violets.
We see countless shades of green.
We see ultraviolet colors
That your naked eye can't see.
But that's enough, you must be frozen
Come and huddle, come and cuddle.
You have neither fur nor feathers.
You'll not last out here alone.

MEW GULL

Even though we're truly humbled
By the others shown before us,
There is something that is special
About our vision, though quite small.

We can't see as far as eagles
Or in water like the penguins.
We don't have an eye for detail
As do vultures on the plain.
And we're awed by all the wonders
Of the silent, deadly owl.

But if They ask you, and They might,
It would please us if you told Them
That our special gift of vision
Is an eye shield from the sun —
Just a cover from the sun.

As with others near the ocean,
Harmful sun rays bounce about us.
Nature's made a sort of cover
That protects our eyes from burning,
That enables us to see.

Nothing more, it's quite that simple
Yet for us it's much like magic.
Just an eye shield, picture maker,
Much like glasses in the sun.

We'd be honored if you'd place us
With the others in your art.

What of humans? What's the reason
That we've not been featured here?

What has happened to our eyesight
That our focus is so narrow,
That we see but what's before us,
And then only in the light?

What about us as you see it?
What has happened to our sight?

SMELL

We are drifters in the night.
You have trembled at our moon call.
In a pack we roam the woods,
And we know that you are present,
Yes, we know you by your scent.

If you're looking for the proof,
Our sense of smell is legendary.
There are those who could convince you
Who aren't here to tell the tale.

There are many who would whisper
That they thought they were well hidden,
But it seems they did not know
Of our prowess in the dark.

They then learned a bitter lesson
That we'd smelt them all these years,
And though you should not be frightened,
We have smelt you all these years.

Yes, we knew that you were present,
Watching deep from in the forest
On a moonlit winter's night.

SMELL

You've observed me in my homeland
From the tundra to the forest.
I survive where others couldn't
And I thrive and rule the north.

I adapt to my surroundings
And my senses are all keen.
And of all that I rely on,
Nothing's sharper than my scent,
None mean more to me than scent.

I don't just hunt in the forest
On a moonlit, quiet night
Where a gentle breeze might tell me
Of a meal that's lost or hiding.
No, I hunt the Rocky Mountains
From the peaks down to the lakes.

Come down to the lake and watch me.
I can show you where to turn
If you're looking for a young moose
Or a deer for your next meal.

I will know because I've smelt him
At a distance far away.
I'll have smelt across the treetops
Ten and twenty miles away.

If they ask you, I'm a mother,
That's the purpose of my life.
It's the thing that keeps me going,
It's my only goal in life.

When our herd is seeking water
And I sense a danger near us,
That's the time you'll see how special
Is the gift I have of scent.

We might be several hundred thousand,
Searching for fresh water;
When the lion slips beside us,
Crouching, waiting for a stray.

I have always and will always
Know my offspring by its scent.
From the time of birth till always,
I will know it by its scent.
In four hundred thousand like it,
I will find it by its scent.

That's my answer and my entry,
That's what scent can do for me.
And I need it more than any,
That's what living means to me.

SMELL

As I step out of my forest,
There are few who know I've left.
As I leave I move unnoticed
Like a breeze above the snow.

My tufted ears and wispy beard
Distinguish me from other cats.
Yet I am here because I know
You're one who seeks the truth.

They know me through my cousins
As sleek and swift and quick and strong.
But have They ever noticed that my
Scent's as keen as any?

Behind my nose there lies a maze
Of bones like no one else here has.
And as I breathe, I draw in air
Across a bank of countless cells
And through this process I decide
To eat or leave disgusted.

And so they say I'm finicky
About the food I choose to eat.
Please show Them that it is the smell
And not the taste that moves me.

As I leave I move unnoticed
Like a breeze above the snow,
And I am here because I know
You're one who seeks the truth.

LYNX

R.S. PARKER '87©

MULE DEER

SMELL

If I'm right that what you seek here
Is the one who needs scent most,
Let me take you for a short time.
Let me take you for a run.

Are you ready for a lesson
Some will find hard to believe?
Do you have the heart to join me?
Can we show Them? Can we teach Them?
Are They open to the magic
That will show the scent I know?
Are you ready? Are you willing?
If you are, then here we go.

Run with me, don't look behind you.
There's a cougar seeking dinner.
Don't stop moving, just keep running.
He will find us if he smells us.
You can trust me, picture maker.
See the water? Ready, leap!
Swim beside me, let Them notice
How this lesson saves our lives.

The thing to notice is our movement
Up the river — yes, upstream.
In a short time, no more odor!
We'll have swum our way upstream.

He won't smell us, he won't find us,
We'll have washed our scent away.
He will think that we have vanished
When we wash our scent away.

What of that then, keen observer,
Will They know what we've just done?
Did it happen? Was it real?
Can They trust me? Do They trust you?

Now I ask you for your judgment:
Have you yet to find my equal?
Have you yet to find another
Who knows smell the way I do?

R.S. PARKER '87 ©

And what about us, what's the reason
That we've not been featured here?

What's happened to our sense of smell,
That's made it dull and useless?
Or has it always been this bleak,
A sense that we now rarely need?

What of us as you see it?
What's happened to our sense of smell?

TOUCH

You've just heard the fleeing mule deer
Speak my name with deep respect.
Did you sense fear in her voice?
Do you feel it? Most here do.

When you speak about my senses,
Will you show Them I can tell
If I'll fit into a crevice
By a twitch upon my whiskers,
By the feeling on my whiskers?

And there's more that They should learn
To understand my sense of touch —
How I feel through my whole body
From my whiskers to my tail,
And to show this you can paint me
As They'd see me on a kill.

First I crouch, then I spring.
Watch my tail sway, that's the secret.
Show it steer me like an arrow,
Show it guide me through the air
Till I land upon my prey.

There I settle on its back,
Grip down deep into its shoulders.
With a mighty tug I snap,
Break its neck from on its shoulders.
They should see its carcass fly:
Twenty feet, that's not unusual.

All this comes from guided flight,
From my tail that leads me to him.
This is what They need to know
To understand my sense of touch.

COUGAR

THREE-TOED SLOTH

I'm the one who's always smiling,
Can you think of why I shouldn't?
There is just so much to dream of
That I'm forced to sleep all day.

I've been hanging here for ages.
(Is this not a branch to die for?)
I've been sleeping eighteen hours
And I'm ready for a nap.

As I slept I dreamt I saw you
In my forest — near my tree.
In my dream you asked me questions
About the power of my touch.

Like some others that you know of,
I have poor sight and poor hearing.
To survive high in the forest,
I am forced to feel for food.

Though my claws are long and deadly,
They are sensitive to touch.
And it's with them that I grope
For tasty leaves or twigs or buds
That I only eat when needed.
Two leaves daily should suffice.
And for water there are dewdrops.
I don't have to move that often.

Please excuse me if I can't stay,
But I'm feeling … somewhat drowsy.
I was going to seek a new branch,
But I think I'll wait till later …
You can stay … but I am fading.
I can…
        hardly…
                stay…

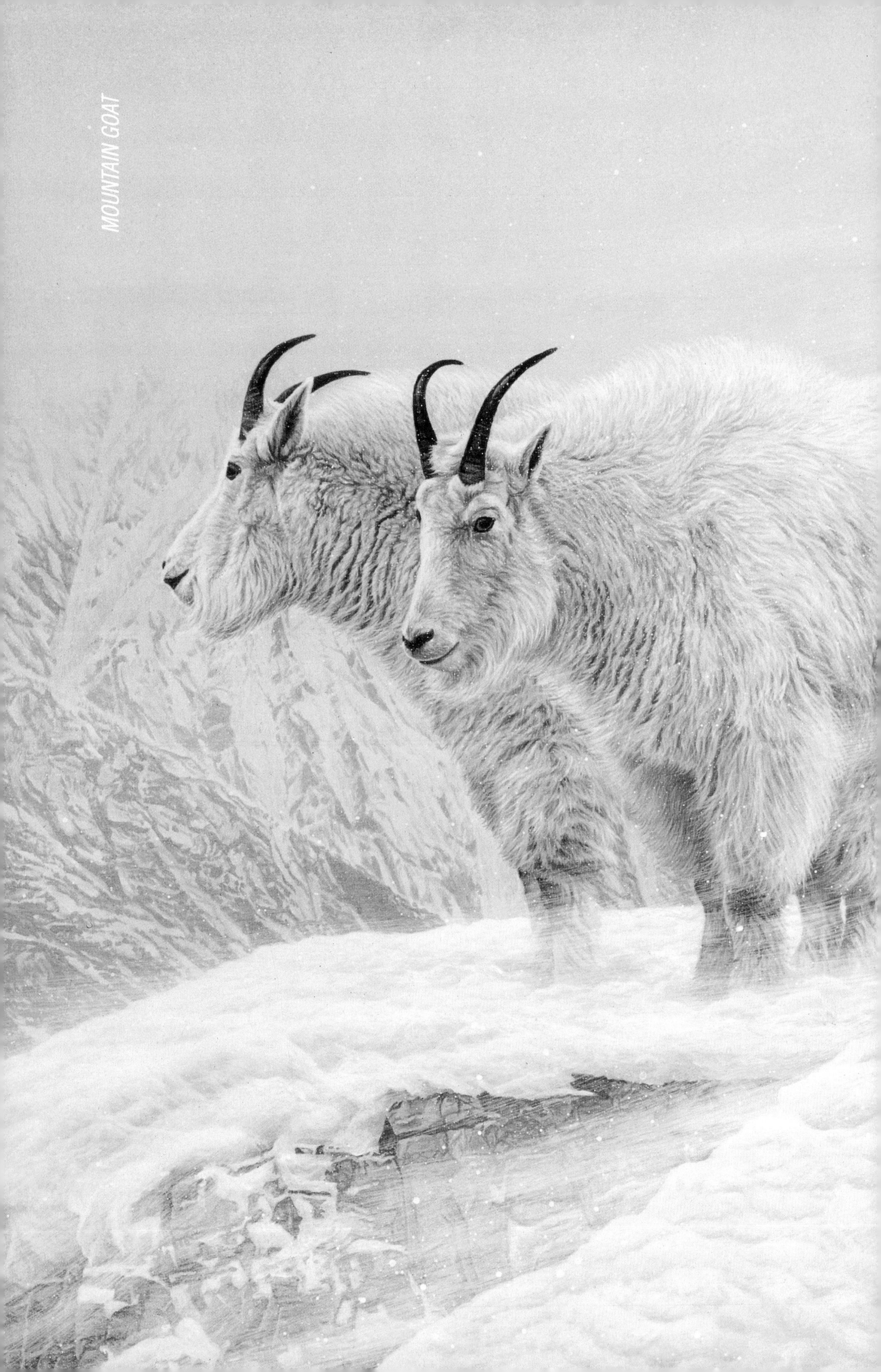

MOUNTAIN GOAT

You've done well to come and find us,
Risked your life to know us better.
Watch your step as you come closer,
There is death down on those rocks.

We have seen you, you're our neighbor,
And we know about your mission:
That you've come to paint what keeps us
High up on these rocky ledges.
Come to see what keeps us standing
High up on the mountain wall.

Now the answer that you're seeking
(And by being here you deserve it),
Is that we don't choose to live here
For the beauty or adventure.
We are much like those below us
Who use all their given senses
To survive and keep on living —
And for us our gift is touch.

There are many who don't know
It's our number one defense.
Where we go, no one can follow.
No one climbs the way we do.
Where we go, you should not follow:
You don't have our gift of touch.

Our broad hooves have sharp crisp edges
That we drive into the mountain,
But that's not the bit of magic
You have come so high to see.

The secret is our hooves are hollow
And they serve as suction cups.
Do They know our hooves are hollow?
This is what you'll want to show Them.
Are there others that you know of
Who depend so much on touch?

RACCOON

R.S. PARKER

I'm here to set the record straight
For those who think they know me well:
My washing habit is a myth!
I've been too long misunderstood!

When They see me, gentle neighbor,
With my two hands in the river,
They see me wash my dinner.
They think I want clean food.

What I do is more than cleaning.
Show Them clearly, make Them see.
Tell Them of my sense of touch,
And how I use my hands as feelers.

When I put my food in water,
That's the way I test its worth.
Is it rotten? Is it wholesome?
This is how I learn the truth.
I don't smell it, I don't taste it,
I just use my hands to feel it.

Show Them why I dunk my food,
And how I use my touch to sense it.
You can help me stop this rumor.
Talk to those who should know better.
You can paint me as you know me,
Paint and show Them why I touch.

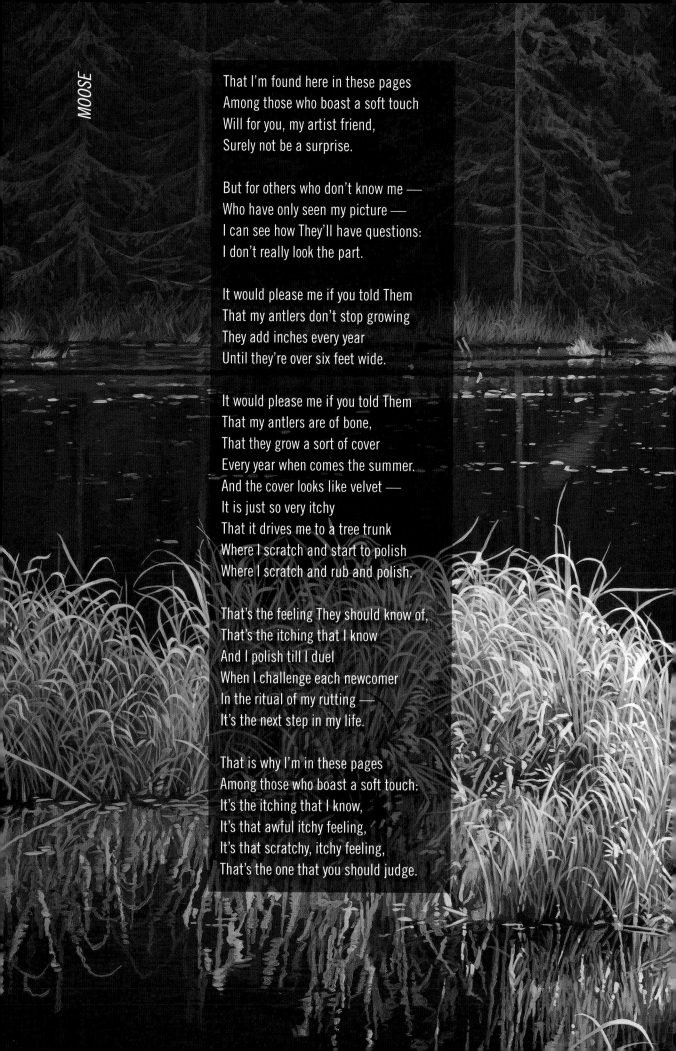

MOOSE

That I'm found here in these pages
Among those who boast a soft touch
Will for you, my artist friend,
Surely not be a surprise.

But for others who don't know me —
Who have only seen my picture —
I can see how They'll have questions:
I don't really look the part.

It would please me if you told Them
That my antlers don't stop growing
They add inches every year
Until they're over six feet wide.

It would please me if you told Them
That my antlers are of bone,
That they grow a sort of cover
Every year when comes the summer.
And the cover looks like velvet —
It is just so very itchy
That it drives me to a tree trunk
Where I scratch and start to polish
Where I scratch and rub and polish.

That's the feeling They should know of,
That's the itching that I know
And I polish till I duel
When I challenge each newcomer
In the ritual of my rutting —
It's the next step in my life.

That is why I'm in these pages
Among those who boast a soft touch:
It's the itching that I know,
It's that awful itchy feeling,
It's that scratchy, itchy feeling,
That's the one that you should judge.

What about us? What's the reason
That we've not been featured here?

What's happened to our sense of touch,
That doesn't seem to serve too much,
Unless we're seeking comfort
In a world that's filled with things?

What about us as you see it?
What has happened to our touch?

HEARING

AFRICAN ELEPHANT

It was early Tuesday morning
When I felt a soft vibration
Somewhere just above my eyebrow,
Not too deep below my skin.

It was early Tuesday morning
That my cousins heard you coming,
When they sent me out a message
One that only I could hear.

As you ponder over hearing
And reflect on how we're special,
Please consider that we hear
Through what's known as "infrasound."

Unlike others, we make low sounds
That we funnel through our noses
And then send out over dense brush
For what could be miles away.

And the sounds we send are *deep* ones
That can pass right through the jungle,
Which is much too thick for high sounds —
Our talk is much like thunder.

"What's that noise? Did you hear it?
Is there danger lurking near?"
"No, it's something from the north ridge.
Yes, it seems they've found fresh water!
We will have to move toward it,
Water's everything out here."

As you ponder over hearing
And consider how we're special,
Why not shut your eyes and listen
For a rumble in the clouds?

VARYING HARE

Crouch way down below the snowbank,
Keep your voice low, please be still.
You will have to whisper softly
If you're here to talk with me.

Like these others, I'm a listener,
With my long ears, hear all comers.
When I'm warned, I do not dally —
At a sound I break and run.

My great ears have other functions.
They can warm me or can cool me.
But for me they're most important
When they help me pick up sounds.

I am sought by just so many,
It is likely I'll die hunted
During the first year of my life.
Odds are in that I won't live
To see a second winter come.

If two like me were left to start
A family with no threats from foes,
Were left alone for three short years,
Can you imagine what you'd find?
If left to breed, and unimpaired,
We would number thirty million.

That's my story. *Keep you head down!*
And the reasons I'm so nervous.
Please be still. *Did you hear that?*

Though my ears are far from mammoth,
I can hear like others can't.
And you can show Them through your pictures,
You can paint me as I am,
Show my movement in the water
How I live and how I hear.

Tell Them of the sounds I make,
The far-off shrills, the whistling cries.
Tell Them of the sounds I send
And how these sounds come back to me.

Tell Them how I hear an echo
Through the melon on my brow,
And with this locate my victim
And all life that swims with me.

Tell Them what I find I eat,
How I hunt and what I eat.
I feed on seals and birds and fish,
And walruses and massive whales.
I feed on anything I choose
And thus I'm known as "killer whale."

They should learn about my hearing
Show Them what you've come to know:
How I keep in touch with others,
How I live and how I hear.

Back to basics, what's your mission?
Size is not the issue here.
Is your query not our hearing?
Are you not out seeking me?

I'm the one, I'm sure you know it,
With the greatest gift of hearing.
They'll agree if you'll just paint me.
Show me listening, show my ears.

During the day, I live in tunnels.
Come the night, I'm on the hunt.
What I hunt is mice and birds,
But that's quite normal, They will say.

What it is that makes me special
Happens when I hunt for insects.
It's in how I come to find them,
Where I find them, when I hear them.

Show Them clearly how it's special.
Show the magic of my hearing.
It is movement that I hear
Underground and not that near.

You can paint me so They notice
That my hearing's truly special.
Will you paint me so They see me?
I'm here listening. I'm all ears!

FOX

R. S. PARKER '86 ©

As you walk along the ocean
And peer out toward the water
And you see a log that's floating —
Look again, it might be me.

Come right down into the harbor,
But be quick, I must keep moving.
I am one the orca's hunting,
And he frequently swims here.

Like the orca, I send signals,
Only mine sound much like clicking.
They bounce back with a clear message:
"Is it time to flee or eat?"

It would serve me if you showed Them
How I dive into the ocean.
How the channels to my ears fill
And then serve me like a drum
That amplifies the slightest sound —
That's how I hear in water.

There's more that makes me special.
I can hear on land as well.
They have surely heard me talking
With my friends out on their shores.

Come and look across your harbor.
I'm here peeking. Can you see me?
Please be quick. I must keep moving.
Now you see me, now you don't.

And what about us? What's the reason
That we've not been featured here?

We will never hear like orcas
or the elephant or hare.
And it's clear we have our limits
When compared to those you love.

What about us as you see it?
What has happened to our hearing?

TASTE

KOALA

R.S. PARKER '88 ©

G'day, mate! I'm here down under
Tickled that I've passed the test.
I've no doubt you could have shown Them
Others near me just as special:
Dingoes, joeys, wombats, possums,
The wallaby or platypus.
Yet I'm here because I'm fussy
That's what makes my taste unique.

They might know I feed on leaves
Of only eucalyptus trees.
And that might seem a simple thing
With hundreds of varieties.

But do They know of all these trees
Just a few are good to eat?
That I must choose among a score.
And even then select the leaves.

And do They know that I don't eat
The new growth from a single tree?

Another thing They'll know me for
Is how I haul my baby.
But do They know that unlike most
My pouch is on my back?

From the treetops I see many
As peculiar as me.
But I am here because I'm fussy —
That's what makes my taste unique.

MINK

R.S. PARKER '8

If your friends come out to find me,
There is little that They'll see.
Just my footprints or my droppings —
Only signs that I was here.

There are lands where many see me
As a trickster, a magician.
Though I'm quite the local hero
In the end, the trick's on me.

For I'm hunted for the luster
And the thickness of my coat.
For its richly shining color
As it changes through the year.

Do They know I often kill
More than just for mere survival?
Do They know what makes me special,
How I hunt most anywhere?

How I'm equally at home
In the cold and dangerous water
Or on land and underground
Where I search for tasty morsels.

Minnows, mice, quick tiny shrews
And my favorite meal the sweet crab.
Where I eat is mine to choose.
I can hunt most anywhere.

If They find me quite elusive,
Tell Them I am "the Magician."
And how if They look real closely,
They'll see signs that I was here.

They'll know me when They see me,
As They've often heard me humming,
Thus the name by which They call me —
And I truly am unique.

I can fly as can no other:
Forward, backward — even hover.
I am quicker than the eye.
None can fly the way I can.

Let them know my quest for sugar
Is what keeps my wings aflutter.
In a world of endless colors
I can always find a prize.

And I'm thankful for the food
That I've found outside your window.
For the nectar's not a mere treat.
It's the source of all my power.

But you know these things about me,
And you've shown it when you paint me.
You have fed me, gentle neighbor.
I have seen how much you care.

RON PARKER '94 ©

I'm known to be the most like you,
My walk, my looks, my senses, too.
Should this likeness not mean something
As you paint me, as you judge me?

My hearing, smell, my sight and touch
Are much the same as yours.
Should this likeness not mean something
As you paint me, as you judge me?

As for the sense that should impress,
I choose to come to you with taste.
Of all the entries seen so far,
None can taste the way you do.
Of all the others that you've painted,
None can taste the way we do.

When offered something new to eat,
Like you I lift it to my nose,
And if it passes, to my mouth
Then slowly down upon my tongue.
Of course I'll eat it if I like it.
But, however, if I don't,
Watch me grimace as I throw it!
Is this not what you would do?

Let Them see how just like Them
I clean my ears, I pick my nose.
I yawn, I burp, I huff and puff
And kiss my babes the way They do.

Does the fact that I'm most like you
Not impress you as you watch me?
Should this likeness not mean something
As you paint me, as you judge me?

LOWLAND GORILLA

I don't care if I am chosen
As the one whose taste is keenest.
Take a look at my expression.
Does it seem as though I care?

Watch the sun beat down upon me,
Or the raindrops fall around me.
I'm so happy just to be here.
There is nothing I don't have.

An old tin can is not a home
That you might care to live in long.
But I know one who seeks it out
And finds it safe and private.

As octopus is warm and snug
And can't imagine any way
That one could get in through the door
Or through the walls — but *I* can!

I tear the lid off with my teeth.
For me it's quite that simple.
For you the answer that you seek
Is found here in this riddle.

The way I'm special if They care,
And you may smile while saying it.
What makes me different from these others
Is my fondness for canned food.

I don't mind if I'm not chosen
As the one whose taste is keenest.
Like so many that you've painted,
I'm just grateful that you care.

R.S. PARKER '84 ©

What of humans, what's the reason
That we're not featured at all?

We, too, possess these senses.
We, too, have strengths ourselves!

What's happened to our eyesight?
That our focus is so narrow
That we see but what's before us
And then only in the light?

What's happened to our sense of smell?
What's made it dull and meaningless?
Or has it always been this bleak,
A sense that we now rarely need?

And what about our sense of touch
That doesn't seem to serve too much
Unless we're seeing comfort in
A world that's filled with things?

We will never hear like orcas
Or the elephant or hare.
And it's clear we have our limits
When compared to those you love.

What if you had ruled on thinking,
Or the sixth sense as we know it?
Might you not have judged us winners?
We have come to rule the planet.
Aren't we champions of the Earth?

What of us in your judgment?
Aren't we showing any changes?
As we come to know these creatures,
Can we look them in the eye?

What of us as you see it?
Are there reasons to start hoping?
As we start to see our limits,
As we grow to share your passion,
As we come to know our senses,
Are we learning how to care?

SIGHT

Bald Eagle *(pages 8–9)*

Eagles can have a wingspan of up to seven and a half feet and are found all over the world, but the bald eagle only lives in North America, where it is found as far south as Florida in the United States. However, 75 percent of America's "national bird" live in Alaska and along Canada's Pacific coast. These two areas usually offer an abundance of salmon, which is the bald eagle's main source of food. Unfortunately, recent declines in salmon stock due to overfishing may have a future impact on the bald eagle as well as other wildlife. This majestic bird, whose numbers in the United States have dropped significantly in the past several years due to industrialism, pollution, and human encroachment, gets its name from its white head.

White-backed Vulture *(pages 10–11)*

Old World vultures, such as the white-backed variety, are related to hawks and eagles, while New World vultures, such as the condor, are distantly related to storks and cormorants. Although it is a predator, the vulture is also a scavenger. Like other vultures, the white-backed variety, found in both Africa and Asia, feeds only on carcasses. Unlike other predators, it does not kill. The vulture's head is naked to prevent its feathers from being fouled during feeding. This bird plays an important role as a natural disposer of carrion. A now-extinct prehistoric vulture had a wingspan of 17 feet. The wingspan of today's Old World vulture doesn't usually exceed seven feet.

Great Horned Owl *(pages 12–13)*

In Europe, Asia, and Africa, the largest of owls is known as the eagle owl. In North America, the great horned is the largest, and possesses similar features to its cousins worldwide: incredible vision in the dark, remarkable hearing, a silent flight (because of the softness of its wings), a hidden beak, and a digestive system that allows it to regurgitate pellets that consist of bones as well as hairs and feathers. The tufts that look like horns on the top of this bird's head are not its ears, which are on either side of the head behind flattened face feathers.

Adélie Penguin *(pages 14–15)*

The penguin is located only in the southern hemisphere, mainly in Antarctica, although some species are found in Australia and New Zealand. The Adélie penguin, which lives in Antarctica, is quite small compared to the emperor penguin, the largest of all penguins at three to four feet in height. Penguins do not eat while on land. They stay alive by subsisting on a layer of fat under their skin and can lose as much as 75 pounds during the two-month period when they incubate their eggs. This flightless bird lives in large colonies which, in Antarctica, can contain as many as half a million birds in 500 acres.

Mew Gull *(pages 16–17)*

Ranging from the Eurasian boreal forest to the Pacific coast of North America, the mew gull, like most gulls, is rarely found far out on the water. Instead, it prefers to stay close to lake and ocean shores. However, the kittiwake, a small oceanic gull, is seldom seen on land, while Franklin's gull, sometimes known as the "prairie dove," is found on the Great Plains of North America. Gulls have long, narrow wings that are adapted to soaring and their feet are webbed so they can swim. With their strong, hooked bills, gulls are able to eat clams and spear fish. However, they often prefer to scavenge in bays and harbors.

SMELL

Wolf *(pages 20–21)*
The gray wolf has been extinct in the British Isles for more than 200 years. However, it still exists in sizable numbers in Continental Europe, particularly in mountainous regions of Italy, the Balkans, and western Russia. The gray wolf is also found throughout much of Asia, especially in Siberia. In North America, this wolf is often called the timber wolf and was once widespread over the entire continent. Today it is largely found from Greenland to the extreme north of the United States, and in a few isolated pockets of wilderness in the American West. Wolves hunt singly or in family groups called packs, which can include as many as five members. Sometimes, during winter, packs join together in larger groups numbering as many as 30 individuals. Efforts are currently being made to restore the wolf to its home in the American Rocky Mountains by capturing and transporting wolves from western Canada, where the animal is still fairly common.

Grizzly Bear *(pages 22–23)*
Found almost exclusively in the northern hemisphere, bears are capable of moving with great speed, as much as 35 miles per hour. Most bears can also climb trees and swim well. The grizzly is among the largest of bears. It can reach lengths of nine feet and weigh as much as 1,700 pounds. In former years the grizzly was found throughout the western half of North America from the Arctic Circle to central Mexico. Today it is almost extinct outside of parks in the United States (with the exception of Alaska) and is found in reduced numbers in the Canadian Rockies, British Columbia, and Yukon Territory. Although a carnivore, the grizzly is also fond of fruit, honey, and insects. The name of this humped bear derives from its grizzled fur.

Blue Wildebeest *(pages 24–25)*
Standing four and a half feet at the shoulder and weighing as much as 500 pounds, the blue wildebeest or brindled gnu is found in southern and eastern Africa. This animal, really a large African antelope, travels in herds through grasslands. They are always on the move in search of new pastures and water, which are in scarce supply in this part of the world. Noted as swift runners, wildebeest engage in elaborate dodging maneuvers to avoid their chief enemy, the lion. A herd of wildebeest can number from 20 to several thousand individuals.

Lynx *(pages 26–27)*
Lynx are found in the northern forests of North America, Europe, and Asia. The European northern lynx is probably extinct in the western part of the continent due to deforestation and continuous human habitation. Its North American cousin, the Canadian lynx, ranges from the northern edge of the Canadian tree line to the extreme northern United States. A nocturnal hunter, the Canadian lynx has longer hair and broader feet (which allow it to walk easily on snow) than its European counterpart. The North American lynx's main source of food is the varying hare, although it will prey on game as large as deer. The bobcat is a smaller variety of lynx with a longer tail, shorter ear tufts, and smaller feet than the Canadian lynx. It is found in thickets, swamps, and rocky areas from southern Canada to central Mexico.

Mule Deer *(pages 28–29)*
Deer are found in most parts of the world except Australia. The only deer in Africa are confined to forested areas in the northern part of that continent where red deer (also native to Europe) are found in small numbers. In North America there are many deer species, the most common being the white-tailed deer. The mule deer is generally found from the Great Plains westward and, unlike other deer, has seen its numbers decline in recent years. This deer is distinguishable by its long mulelike ears and black-tipped tail. At one time the white-tailed deer was nearly exterminated due to overhunting. Nowadays, though, there are fears that this deer has become too numerous, especially since its natural predator, the wolf, has almost disappeared in the United States and the more urbanized regions of Canada.

TOUCH

Cougar *(pages 32–33)*
The largest North American cat goes by the name of cougar, puma, painter, catamount, panther, and mountain lion. Although it once roamed freely across North, Central, and South America, today, in North America, it is generally restricted to the western part of the continent. However, some cougars can still be found in Florida. Despite their popular reputation for fierceness, cougars avoid contact with humans and rarely attack them. Their favorite prey are deer. Adult male cougars can reach lengths of seven feet and weigh more than 175 pounds; females are smaller.

Three-toes Sloth *(pages 34–35)*
Distantly related to armadillos and anteaters, sloths live in Central and South American rainforests where they sleep, eat, and travel in the trees. The three-toed sloth (which has three toes on its front feet and five on it hind feet) is slightly smaller than its two-toed cousin, but both species have algae-covered fur that acts as a greenish camouflage in the forest. Sloths spend most of their active life hanging from branches by their long claws and move through the trees at a top speed of about one mile per hour. Still, this sluggish animal can move swiftly and powerfully if threatened. The three-toed sloth is about the size of a house cat and feeds almost exclusively on the leaves, buds, and stems of a tropical relative of the mulberry tree.

Mountain Goat *(pages 36–37)*
Although not a true goat, this native of the high mountains in southeast Alaska, western Canada, and the northwestern United States belongs to the same family and is goatlike in appearance. Related to the chamois of Eurasia, the mountain goat lives in small herds on steep mountainsides and cliffs where it feeds on stunted vegetation above the timberline. Like the chamois, the mountain goat is a lively climbing animal distinguished from sheep by its smaller head, bearded chin (in the male), and its short, upturned tail. A male mountain goat can stand three and a half feet at the shoulder and weigh as much as 300 pounds.

Raccoon *(pages 38–39)*
The raccoon is the ultimate nocturnal animal. It is aquatic and arboreal, which means it is as capable in the water as it is in the trees. Ranging from southern Canada to South America, except in parts of the Rocky Mountains and in deserts, the raccoon prefers to live close to water. It eats almost anything, including nuts, seeds, fruits, eggs, insects, frogs, and crayfish, which are perhaps it favorite food. Unlike many animals, raccoons seem to thrive in urban areas and are often found in large numbers in cities where they feast on garbage and can be something of a nuisance.

Moose *(pages 40–41)*
Found in the northern part of North America and Eurasia, this largest member of the deer family narrowly escaped extinction in the last century. Today it is protected in North America in national parks and reserves, while in Eurasia (where it is usually known as an "elk") it ranges from Scandinavia to eastern Siberia. The largest variety of moose, the adult male Alaska, can weigh from 1,000 to 1,800 pounds, stand seven and a half feet at the shoulder, and have an antler spread of up to six feet. Moose eat leaves, twigs, buds, and the bark of some woody plants, as well as lichens and aquatic plants. Known as strong swimmers, moose have reportedly crossed lakes that are many miles wide.

HEARING

African Elephant *(pages 44–45)*
The African elephant, the largest living land mammal, is found south of the Sahara Desert and is distinguishable from its Indian counterpart by its larger size, its larger ears and tusks (the largest teeth of any animal), and by its sloping head. It also has a shorter life expectancy, 50 compared to 70 years, than its Indian cousin. The African elephant once lived in most of Africa, but war, human encroachment, drought, and widespread hunting have severely reduced its numbers and range. Continued poaching for its much-valued ivory tusks is recognized as such a serious problem that many environmentalists feel that the African elephant may soon become extinct in the wild unless drastic measures are taken. Today this highly intelligent and social animal lives mainly in reserves in central and southern Africa.

Varying Hare *(pages 46–47)*
Hares generally have longer ears and hind legs than rabbits and travel by jumping rather than by running. Ranging in weight from three to 13 pounds and in length from 13 to 25 inches, hares are native to Europe, Asia, Africa, and North and Central America. In recent times they have been introduced into Australia where, like rabbits, they have flourished all too well. The varying hare, sometimes known as the snowshoe hare, is commonly found in the woodlands of the northern part of North America. It was given the nickname "snowshoe" because of the thick hair that it grows on its feet in the winter to enable it to travel easily in the snow. Its real name, varying hare, is dues to its ability to change color from brown in the summer to white in the winter. Like all hares and rabbits, the varying hare has a multitude of enemies, and its chief means of continued survival is its extraordinary fertility. When danger is near, hares warn other hares by thumping on the ground with their hind legs.

Orca *(pages 48–49)*
This largest member of the dolphin family is truly king of the seas. Male orcas can reach a length of 30 feet, while females are half that size. Found all over the world, orcas, or killer whales, hunt everything from fish and birds to walruses and porpoises. Armed with more than four dozen very sharp teeth, this creature, in packs, will even take on the largest of whales. And yet orcas are extremely social mammals, living with family members in pods that can contain from two to 50 individuals. Today this well-known sea mammal is the subject of a worldwide debate over the morality of maintaining it in captivity, particularly in marine parks and zoos.

Fox *(pages 50–51)*
The fox, like its larger cousin the wolf, is a member of the dog family, and is found throughout most of the northern hemisphere. Unlike most members of the dog family, which run down their prey, foxes frequently hunt by stalking and pouncing, much as a cougar would. The kit fox usually makes its home in the deserts of North America. Due to excessive trapping and poisoning, this fox has seen its numbers greatly diminish to the point where it has become rare in many parts of its range. The kit fox lives in holes and, like most foxes, is nocturnal. In the dark of the night it uses its large ears to listen for and track down its prey.

Harbor Seal *(pages 52–53)*
The harbor, or common, seal lives predominantly in the North pacific and North Atlantic but can be found as far south as California. It is monogamous and is usually found in large schools, lying on a rocky or sandy beach on the lookout for its greatest enemy, the killer whale. Tears are often seen running down its cheeks when it is on land. This is by no means an indication of its emotional state. The tears are produced naturally to lubricate its eyes until it returns to the water. Some seals, particularly the harp and the ring, have long been hunted by humans for food, oil, and hides. Although not regulated by international treaties, the hunting of seals in still quite controversial, especially that of harp seals off Canada's Atlantic coast.

TASTE

Koala *(pages 56–57)*

This cuddly little Australian marsupial, or pouched animal, was hunted to such an extent at the beginning of this century that two national parks had to be created to save it from extinction. The koala was hunted chiefly for its fur. Disease and the destruction of Australia's eucalyptus forests have also contributed to the koala's decline in numbers. Today the animal, which is not related to the bear at all, is found primarily in Queensland, Victoria, and New South Wales. Nocturnal and slow-moving, the koala first emerges from its mother's pouch at about six months. Until it is eight months old, it continues to ride in the pouch and then, roughly four months later, it is carried on its mother's back or in her arms.

Mink *(pages 58–59)*

Related to the weasel, minks are native to North America, some parts of Europe (mostly Russia), and central Asia. Minks have never existed in Great Britain or Iceland, but animals that have escaped from mink farms have now established wild populations in those countries. The North American mink, at 20 to 28 inches long (including its seven– to nine–inch tail), is much larger than its European cousin. Its coat, too, is thicker and softer, which makes it more important to the fur industry, both in America and in Europe. Today, however, most of the mink used in the fur trade comes from animals bred and raised on farms, where many colors have been produced.

Rufous Hummingbird *(pages 60–61)*

Varying in size from the two-and-one-quarter-inch fairy hummingbird of Cuba to the eight-and-one-half-inch giant hummer of the Andes Mountains in South America, this energetic bird is only found in the New World. Hummingbirds can fly as fast as 60 miles per hour, but their weak feet can't support them on flat surfaces. In order to expend the incredible energy that they do, this tiny bird must feed continuously, and at night they fall into a sleeping state not unlike an animal in hibernation. At maximum speed the hummingbird's wing beats are so rapid (50 to 75 beats per second) that the human eye sees the wings as a blur. No other hummingbird lives as far north as does the rufous. Like its cousin the ruby-throated hummer, the rufous migrates annually to Mexico and Central America for the winter. As with most species of hummingbirds, the rufous (reddish-brown) derives its name from its color.

Lowland Gorilla *(pages 62–63)*

The largest of the great apes can stand up to six feet and can weigh more than 400 pounds. The lowland gorilla lives in the rainforests of western and central equatorial Africa. They number about 90,000, while their cousins, the mountain gorillas, are almost extinct, barely numbering a few hundred in the mountainous regions of Rwanda, Zaire, and Uganda. Despite their appearance and occasional aggressive manner, gorillas are vegetarians. They eat a variety of vines, leaves, berries, roots, and bark. This impressive animal generally relies on bluffs — roaring and beating its chest — to scare off intruders. Human poachers are its principal enemy.

Sea Otter *(pages 64–65)*

Found in and around the kelp beds of the North Pacific, the sea otter, a member of the muskrat family, swims on its back, carrying its cub and eating its meals of abalone, crab, and sea urchin. This playful animal is fond of using rocks to smash open shellfish, and is equally adept at ripping apart discarded soft drink cans that often house small octopuses. At one time, this plentiful marine mammal nearly became extinct due to overhunting by fur traders. Today, although now protected by international agreement, sea otters are still threatened by oil spills off Alaska's shores. The oil from spills causes hypothermia by destroying the insulating properties of the animal's beautiful pelt.